Wiggle! Woggle!

Written by Alison Hawes

Illustrated by Tania Konstant

My tooth is wiggly.

3

I show it to Mum.

5

I show it to Megan.

My tooth comes out!

I put it in an envelope.

I put it under my pillow.

I get a surprise!

13

I get a **new** toothbrush...

for my **new** tooth!